A MODERN FABLE

A MODERN FABLE

Jim Schembri

Angus&Robertson
An imprint of HarperCollins*Publishers*

Angus & Robertson
An imprint of HarperCollins*Publishers* (Australia) Pty Ltd
(ACN 008 431 730)

HarperCollins*Publishers*
25 Ryde Road Pymble, Sydney NSW 2073
22–24 Joseph Street North Blackburn, Melbourne VIC 3130
31 View Road, Auckland 10, New Zealand

Copyright © Jim Schembri 1995

All rights reserved. Except as provided by Australian copyright law, no part of this book may be reproduced without permission in writing from the publisher.

First published 1995
Text design and cover typography by Jo Waite
Cover illustration and design by Liz Dixon
Text illustrations by Liz Dixon
Typeset in 10.5/13pt Raleigh by J&M Typesetting
Produced by HarperCollins*Publishers*, Hong Kong

The National Library of Australia
Cataloguing-in-Publication data:

Schembri, Jim, 1962–.
  A modern fable.

  ISBN 0 207 18906 4.

  1. Australian essays – 20th century. I. Title. II. Title:
  Age (Melbourne, Vic.).

A824.3

Contents

Introduction	VII
The old tree	1
The boy on the edge of the pier	3
Kevin the lost Cruise missile	5
Bernie and his time-share soul	7
An almost perfect life	9
The good-memory girl	11
The urban terrorist	13
RSVP	15
Poor timing	17
The editing suite	19
Frannie's franchise	21
Natural talents	23
The last blip	25
Fidgety digits	27
Engine trouble	29
Glass of water	31
The princess who wanted a life	32
The men who let it rain	34
CyberChrist	36
The artist and the executive	38
The philosopher who was full of it	39

LITTLE RULES	41
THE WISE OLD WOMAN WHO WOULDN'T BE TOLD	43
TERRORIST OF LOVE	45
PHIL JUNIOR OF FLYLAND	46
MODERN FRIENDS	48
SEVEN SHORT NAKED MEN	50
THE BEAST AND THE LEASH	52
MRS OCTOPUS GETS DOWN TO BUSINESS	54
THE HUG OF DOOM	56
THE DIAMOND KEYRING THAT WENT FOR A SWIM	58
JASPER'S BIG TRIP	60
THE LOLLIPOP ANGEL	62
REVALUING THE CONTENTS OF ROBBIE'S HEAD	64
EDDIE AND THE CANYON	66
UPRIGHT AND UPTIGHT IN THE LAND OF NOD	68
THE LIFE OF THE LINGS	70
THE WOODPECKER AND THE TREE	72
DRAGON FRIEND	74
THE TALE OF SPITEFUL BRETT	76
SQUIRKY GETS READY	78
VAL AND VIN GO FOR A SPIN	80
PLANET HOPE	82
THE OLD MAN AT THE LIGHTS	84
A DAY AT THE ZOO	86
THE CUTE, FURRY POSSUM TWINS	88
THE STARVING SHARKS	90
THE MEMORY TEST	92
THE SYMPATHY SHOP	94
THE RAGGED GIRL AND THE ROCK	96
CHELSEA STARLET'S RESTING PLACE	98
WHAT THE GNU KNEW	100

Introduction

Many years ago, humans first crawled out of the primordial slime, took a look around, flipped a coin, and decided to invent society rather than crawl back in.

Since then, fables have told of the intricacies, frailties and stupidities of human nature. Writers such as Aesop and La Fontaine used animal rather than human characters to tell their stories and always ended them with a neat moral.

However these fables were written a long time ago when life was simpler and nobody had to spend half their afternoon struggling with a malfunctioning fax machine, or wondering why the person they've known for twenty years has suddenly stopped returning calls.

As we stumble through the age of the sound byte, the mobile phone, high-tech weaponry, satellite surveillance, micro-chips, potato chips, short attention spans and artificial sweeteners, the stories in *A Modern Fable* look at where we are as a species, and where we might be going.

From the big questions – why are we here? – to the bigger questions – we know why we're here, now how do we get to somewhere with a better view? – this collection of modern fables offers an often humorous, sometimes dark, occasionally piercing insight into the human condition and its strange by-product, civilization.

The Old Tree

The big forest that had stood for a thousand years was going to be chopped down to make way for the new city. The plans had all been made, the trees had all been marked.

A lot of the people who would be doing the chopping and sawing felt sorry for the trees they had to cut down, knowing full well how long they had been alive. But they thought of the happiness the new city would bring to the people who would live and work in it for years to come.

But one person did not want the forest cut down. She said the city had no right to sacrifice something so old and so beautiful just so another city, with all its noise and pollution, could be built. The tree cutters told this person that the city would be clean and good for all, but she did not believe them.

As the tree cutters moved through the forest, the woman pleaded with them to stop because they were killing something very special.

"We have to do this," they explained to her, before moving her aside to continue the cutting.

Feeling helpless, the woman cried and cried. Then she decided to find the oldest tree left in the forest and save it, so the people of the new city would have a symbol to remind them of all that is old and wise and beautiful in nature.

The woman chained herself to the old tree and swallowed the key. The tree cutters could not persuade her to move so they left the old tree alone and cut down the rest of the forest.

Only when the plans for the roads and buildings and factories of the new city had made room for the old tree did the woman allow herself to be freed.

And so the new city was built around the grand old tree, which now stood as the last towering vestige of the forest that had once stood there. The woman looked with pride at what she had achieved, and left to save other trees.

Twenty years later the woman returned to the new city. It was now old and dirty and full of people sick from the foul smoke of its industry and traffic. But the old tree still stood, high and alone, amid the pollution and noise.

"See what I have done for you," the woman said to the tree. "Because of me you have survived to see the folly of progress, to witness the grandeur of your own existence."

"I knew that already," said the tree. "Why didn't you just let me die?"

THE BOY ON THE EDGE OF THE PIER

When Tommy was a little boy he used to go fishing every Saturday afternoon. He would sit on the end of the long pier near the house in the cold coastal town where he lived. He would drop his line into the water and hope that a fish would take.

All the other young boys and girls also went fishing on Saturday afternoon, but they did not sit on the same pier as Tommy. They sat on the short pier a little way down from Tommy. They did this because this is where all the fish were.

The long pier, where Tommy always went, never seemed to have any fish near it at all. But Tommy kept going there, hoping. "Come and fish with us," the boys and girls would often say to Tommy. "You won't catch anything there. Come and fish with us."

"No," Tommy would say proudly. "I want to catch fish here and I want to catch them by myself."

In time, the boys and girls and Tommy grew up. Some of them left the town, saying it was too small and windy and cold. But many stayed and turned fishing into a great industry which brought much fame and prosperity to the town. Many of those who had left returned, and were welcomed.

But Tommy kept fishing from the long pier, catching nothing. As the others rode out to sea in their huge, modern fishing trawlers, they would see Tommy sitting on the edge of the pier.

"Why don't you join us?" they would ask. "There is plenty for everyone. We just want you to share with us."

"I shall catch fish here and I shall catch them by myself," Tommy said.

Early one morning someone pulled up alongside Tommy in her boat. "How can you live on nothing?" she wanted to know. "What do you give to your family, your friends, to people who come over?"

"I have no family. I have no friends. And no one ever comes over," Tommy said.

"No one ever comes over because you don't let us," she said. Then she sped off to join the rest of the fishing fleet.

Late that afternoon as the boats returned some people noticed that Tommy was lying on the pier. They found that he was dead. But his hands were still tightly gripping the rod. They saw that something was tugging at the line. They looked over the edge of the pier into the water. On the other end of Tommy's fishing line was the biggest fish they had ever seen.

The doctors later found that Tommy had died of shock.

KEVIN THE LOST CRUISE MISSILE

Kevin the Cruise missile was hopelessly lost. He was not supposed to get lost. He had a very sophisticated navigational guidance system designed to take him directly to his target, however small or far away it was. He even had a flashing red light that would stop flashing once he reached his target.

But while flying very low below the radar nets Kevin somehow lost his way. He turned this way and that, through valleys, over mountain ranges, across oceans, deserts and polar icecaps, but he could not regain his bearings.

He soon came across a small village. Kevin thought to himself: "Aha, I've finally found my target." But the little red light kept flashing. So he flew on.

He came across a large industrial complex. "Aha! This must be where I'm supposed to go." But the little red light kept flashing. So on he flew.

Kevin tried many targets of opportunity, but each time he got them in his cross hairs he would look at the little red light, which would still be flashing. So he would fly past.

Kevin wandered for months and years. Eventually he ran into Julie, another lost Cruise missile. They ran into Raymond, who had the same problem. Before long they were joined by Geoff, Sammy, Deidre, Frank, Cindy, Beatrice, Lindy, Chamsy, Terri, Martin and Warren.

They all flew around together, lost, lonely, unwanted, looking for a place to call ground zero. They felt bad, but at least they were in a group.

One day Kevin politely asked everyone if they thought this was a waste of time. Everyone quickly agreed. So they took a vote and decided they should shed their warheads and just stick together. This made them feel much better.

Kevin looked at the little red light. It had stopped flashing.

BERNIE AND HIS TIME-SHARE SOUL

Bernie was shocked when he got to Hell. Waiting for him at the bottom of the escalator was Satan, the Prince of Darkness, who wanted to buy Bernie's soul.

"I thought you owned it already," said Bernie. "I've killed, lied and cheated, not believing in anything but myself."

"You have been bad," said Satan as he led Bernie into his office. "But your soul is still yours. And I want it."

"Huh?" said Bernie.

Satan sat Bernie down and poured him a drink. "Bern, I can keep you down here shovelling coal into the eternal furnace until this place freezes over. But how would you like another go at life?"

"Huh?" said Bernie.

"Think about this, Bern. People up there go on and on about the importance of the soul. But you add up the time the average person spends actually using their soul. You'd be lucky if you had more than a minute on the clock."

"Hmm," said Bernie.

"What good is a soul if you're going to spend so little time using the thing? Sell it to me in exchange for a new life.

Now don't tell me that ain't the bargain of the week, and it's not like it's some huge sacrifice."

"Hmm," said Bernie.

"Look, don't worry about the details. Just sign here and I'll have you back on the street before lunch."

"So what do you get out of it?" Bernie asked as he signed, not quite understanding but knowing a good deal when he saw it.

"Just the satisfaction of knowing I'm right," Satan said, sending Bernie back to life.

An Almost Perfect Life

Morty and Margy loved each other very much but they did not love the rat race their success and money had put them in. They were sick of telephones and answering machines and faxes and press releases and meetings and corporate ladders and television programming and digital alarm clocks and beepers and pollution and cars and industry and noise and most of the people they knew.

They wanted to leave the rat race, but they did not want to leave it all because there were bits of it they liked. "We're going to have our cake and eat it too," they said.

So they made their own Utopia. They bought a small island far away in the middle of a big ocean and built their dream home.

They had no fax machine or mailing address, but they had a phone that could only call out. They had no newspapers, but they had a short-wave radio. They had no money, but they kept their high-yielding stock holdings. They had no television antennae or satellite dish, but they had a TV monitor and a VCR so they could watch their favorite movies and TV shows again and again and again. They grew their own food.

Morty and Margy were also careful not to hurt any of the friends and relatives they left behind. They promised to phone once every few months. And if an emergency cropped up, their lawyer had a sealed envelope with the longitude and latitude of their island which could be opened only in very specific circumstances.

Morty and Margy worked hard to have the best of both worlds – their own and everyone else's. And they did it.

But one day while they were lying on the golden sands of their perfect beach, looking into each other's eyes and falling deeper and deeper in love, a nuclear explosion rocked an atoll nearby. Illegal atomic testing was happening there. Then an oil slick from a damaged tanker ruined their coastline. Then airliners began dumping sewage on them.

"Well, this certainly proves something, doesn't it?" said Morty.

"Yeah," said Margy. "No matter how hard you try to live a full and happy and moral life and do right by people and right by yourself, ploppy things still happen."

THE GOOD-MEMORY GIRL

Jenny could spot the flaws in every person she met. She wasn't a cynic, or nasty or mean-spirited or even bitchy – she was just a good judge of character.

Jenny saw through people who were trying to be something they weren't. She could tell when people were simply being who they were. And people could tell she could tell.

This was good because it kept Jenny from getting into bad relationships, especially with men. This was something all her girlfriends seemed to do at one time or another, no matter how careful they thought they were.

And Jenny was honest. She would say what she thought to people's faces, no matter how much it hurt them. And she did not seem to mind.

"That is the price you pay for honesty," she would say.

Some people hated her, but respected her judgment. Some people liked her, but liked her only so much. But everyone sought her advice because Jenny could spot the flaws in every person she met.

Then one day a piano fell on her head. Luckily it was only a toy piano, but it was still enough to knock Jenny out and put her in a deep coma.

She lay asleep for weeks and weeks and months and months. When she finally came to, her brain was found to be damaged in such a way that now she could see and remember only the good in people.

She became very popular from then on. She had absolutely no credibility when it came to judging people's character, but nobody really seemed to mind.

THE URBAN TERRORIST

The tiny country of Sindo Sindo had lived in peace for 3000 years. It had no crime, no violence, no trouble. There were no guns. It had no police and no army to defend itself for it did not need them.

Providence and clever government saw that Sindo Sindo had no natural resources, industry or trade links that would invite hostility from other countries. The place was of no value to anyone except those who lived there.

But slowly and sadly Sindo Sindo became the most cost-effective terrorist target in the world.

"We must do something," said the president to her people. "We are peaceful, but if we do nothing to defend ourselves everything we value will be destroyed."

Everyone agreed. So they hired a Man much skilled in the weapons and ways of war.

On his first day he went to a skyscraper where a sniper was shooting people in the name of his god. The Man killed him.

There was a grand ceremony. The Man was asked to speak, but said nothing.

The next day he went to the airport, where a woman wanted to blow up an airplane full of people for world peace. Without hurting one passenger, the Man killed her.

There was another ceremony. The Man was again asked to speak, but said nothing.

The next day he went to a secret hideout in the hills. This was the headquarters of the terrorists. He went in and killed them all.

There was another grand ceremony, at which the Man was heralded for ridding Sindo Sindo of violence and allowing the people to go back to the way they were before. They again asked him to speak.

This time the Man spoke. "I am a killer," he said. "And so are each of you."

They made not a sound, for they knew he was right.

R S V P

Larry lived in a huge desolate wasteland. The wind was harsh, as were the rain and the sun. The ground was hard and featureless. Larry had no company, not even his shadow, for when the sun was out, it burned directly above him.

During the day he could see forever and see nothing. During the night it was pitch black and he saw the same. All he could do was endure – and walk.

In time he came across a room. There was a party going on. People were dancing, laughing, joking, drinking, having a great time. Larry watched from a distance. No one ever went in and no one ever came out. It never seemed to stop or even slow down.

Larry began thinking what it would be like to be at the party. "Wouldn't it be nice to be the bartender in there, or the drinks waiter or even the hat-check person or the toilet attendant," he thought.

So one night Larry tried to force one of the windows to open. It wouldn't. He tried to smash the glass. He couldn't. He tried to get the people inside to see him. They didn't. He even climbed onto the roof to pry open a hole. He fell.

Larry then tried tunnelling, but the ground was too hard. He was about to give up and move on when two bouncers with big, strong hands grabbed him and took him to the doorman.

"Larry, isn't it?" said the doorman, checking his name off the doorlist. "We've been expecting you."

"But what about the dress code?" Larry said, pointing to the big sign that said: FORMAL DRESS ONLY: NO THONGS, SINGLETS OR SHORTS.

"That's okay," said one of the bouncers. "We'll take care of you."

So they washed and dressed him and sent him to the wonderful party hostess.

"Where have you been?" she said, kissing him and taking his arm. "Now the party can really get started."

Larry pinched himself. It only hurt.

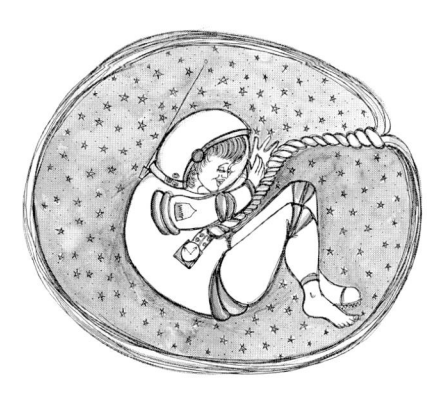

POOR TIMING

Susan was examining one of the rear panels of the spaceship that had come loose during a recent micro-meteor shower. She did not like leaving the spaceship, it was too dangerous. Besides, she had enough to worry about. But it was her turn to do the EVA (extra-vehicular activity) so she reluctantly put on her spacesuit and left the ship.

As she pulled the panel back to inspect the damage, a fuel cylinder exploded. The force of the silent blast tore through the safety cord that tied Susan to the ship, ruptured her oxygen line and sent her hurtling into deepest space.

Within seconds the spaceship disappeared from Susan's view and the planet it was orbiting grew smaller and smaller until it was just a pinprick of light among thousands of other pinpricks of light.

Susan's suit was bleeding oxygen. She looked at her gauge. She had three minutes left. She tried calling the ship for help but her communicator had been damaged in the explosion. So, helpless, Susan vanished at terrific speed into the darkest reaches of the universe.

She did not know if the others would come and rescue her. The chances were very slim. At first Susan panicked. Then she realised she was free. Her debts, her family problems, her reputation were not worries any more. In fact, she would probably be forgiven her sins and be made a hero.

She looked around at the magnificent starscapes that entombed her. Susan was in bliss.

But the others came.

THE EDITING SUITE

Neddy died a quiet death. Then he went not quite to Heaven. He found himself in a room full of switches and dials and gadgets and screens. Then an Angel appeared.

Her name was Freda.

"What is this place?" said Neddy to Freda.

"This is the place where you edit your life," said Freda. She reached in under her wing and pulled out a large spool of film. "This is the film of your life. Every moment, every thought, every deed, good and bad."

Neddy felt cold, even though he was already dead.

"But it is too long," said Freda the Angel. "So we will let you cut it down on this machine here." Freda showed Neddy how the special editing desk worked. She taught Neddy how to add music, do lap dissolves, split screens and other special effects. She then gave Neddy a big black bin in which to throw the discarded footage.

"How long can I make it?" asked Neddy, very politely.

"Normal feature-film length will do," said Freda the Angel. "And take your time. You've got plenty of it. Remember, you're in Eternity now. So do a good job." Then Freda the Angel left.

Neddy couldn't believe his luck. He got straight to work cutting and splicing his life and rapidly compiled what he thought was a fair picture of himself. When he finished, not too long after, he buzzed Freda the Angel.

"Here is my life," said Neddy proudly, presenting her with the final cut reel. "Tight and well-paced and all told in ninety-eight minutes."

"You keep it," said Freda the Angel as she picked up the big black bin. "We judge by the off-cuts."

FRANNIE'S FRANCHISE

One cold, cold day in the heartless heart of the big, big city, a woman called Frannie sat on a chair in the middle of the square under a sign that read: FREE HUGS.

On the first day business was slow. This was because people were suspicious. "What is she really up to?" they asked themselves. "Why is it free? What's in it for her? What's in it for me? Do I have to sign anything? Is the whole thing being secretly filmed?"

Frannie quickly sensed what was wrong. So the next day she changed the sign. It now read:

FREE HUGS
NO STRINGS ATTACHED
NO QUESTIONS ASKED

Business picked up after that. People lined up around the block. Late one night as Frannie prepared to go home after a busy day's work a man went up to her.

"It's quite a nice little racket you've got there," he said.

"It's not a racket," she said. "I'm just helping people a bit."

"You could help them a lot more, you know."

"Oh?" she said, hiding her smile. "How?"

"By charging. Turn a profit, expand, set up franchises worldwide. A staff of thousands servicing millions of people. Imagine the potential!" His mouth began to foam. "Then, diversify! Mini-hugs. Mega-hugs. Family hugs. Discount hugs. Hug Starter Incentive Programs. Hug vouchers, redeemable at any Hug Booth." His eyes nearly popped. "We'll patent the concept. If people hug on their own, we'll sue! For squillions! We'll be rich!"

Exhilarated and exhausted, the man doubled over to catch his breath. Frannie was going to say "If I was doing this for money, I wouldn't be doing this." Instead, she hugged him.

He got the point.

NATURAL TALENTS

Stan the stick insect was in trouble. A big ugly bug-eating monster wanted him for breakfast and was chasing him through the forest. If Stan had had wings he would have flown to safety. If he had had legs that were less awkward and gangling, he would have run faster. If he had had a stronger body he would have fought back. But all he could do was run.

Stan soon found himself trapped at the edge of a pond. The bug monster was closing fast and was in no mood for negotiation. So, in a blind panic, Stan threw himself into the pond. To his great surprise, he found that because of the very things that made him weak – his light body and long thin legs – he was able to walk on the water. This was due to a scientific phenomenon called Surface Tension. (But Stan just thought it was magic.)

Stan walked to the middle of the pond, so that when the big ugly bug eater arrived, he was well out of reach. The bug eater tried swimming after Stan, but nearly drowned, her species not being natural swimmers. The monster scurried back to land and left in a huff to find less troublesome bugs to eat.

Stan felt great. He could now blissfully eat and enjoy life. Whenever a bug eater came after him, he simply ran back to the pond, which he was never far from, and walked across the water to safety.

Stan even began taunting the monsters from the middle of the pond, secure in the knowledge that their species had no affinity with water.

One day Stan was feeding happily when a bug monster came after him. Stan casually hopped onto the pond and skated to the middle where, to his shock, he began to sink. He had put on far too much weight through good living for the surface tension to sustain him. (Stan didn't know this, of course. He just thought the magic had worn off.)

So Stan sank to the bottom where, waiting for him with its mouth wide open, was Gerald, the first of a new strain of big ugly bug-eating monsters who had adapted to water. Gerald had grown fat on Stans.

THE LAST BLIP

The new leader of the world was furious. "I'm glad to be putting all you people out of work," she said to the thousands of scientists assembled before her. "You have spent hundreds of years and billions of dollars searching space for signs of intelligent life while people on Earth went hungry and homeless. You should all hang your heads in shame!"

And they did, for none of the signals they sent out ever received a reply. For a long time the scientists had argued passionately that the search was important for the development of the human soul, and each time the argument won funds.

But a new world leader had been elected, promising less extravagance and more social justice. Thus the scientists lost their jobs.

So a huge team of computer de-programmers began erasing all the data and unplugging all the equipment that had been used in the search. It was all to be sold to feed the hungry and house the homeless.

On the last night of the operation, the last de-programmer left working was about to disconnect the very last of the hundreds of radio telescopes that had been devoted to the search when a small blip appeared on a computer screen. It was a reply from space. The computer decoded the signal. It said simply: "Yes? Hello?"

Before the de-programmer allowed herself too much time to think, she did everyone a favor. She pulled the plug and kept quiet.

FIDGETY DIGITS

No matter how many times Harry hit his keyboard, his screen remained dead. Everyone else in the office was having the same problem. Everyone else in the world was having the same problem.

None of the banks worked. None of the corporations worked. None of the weapons systems worked. Communication networks fell silent. Industry stood still.

For five long minutes the world was frozen in chaos. Airplanes crashed. Cars collided. Many died. Then everything came back on. The governments of the world tried to find out what had happened, but couldn't.

When Harry went home he told his wife and young daughter. They watched the TV to see if the cause had been found. Many had theories. Some said it might be something from space, but nobody knew for sure.

Late that night, Harry's daughter woke him up. She told Harry a tale of how she was leading the children of the world to unite by using the computers their parents had bought them. She told Harry that what had happened that day would happen again tomorrow at a precise time. Harry got up, took his daughter to the kitchen, gave her a cool glass of water, then tucked her into bed and kissed her goodnight.

The next day it did happen again. The world stopped.

Harry looked at his watch. His daughter was right. The children had taken over.

"What are you going to do?" he asked his daughter.

"We are going to run everything, we are going to fix everything."

"But you can't," said Harry, although he knew he was wrong. His daughter knew this, too.

"You can't blame us for doing it," said Harry's daughter. "You gave us the power. We used what you gave. That's all."

"But when we bought them for you, we thought they were just toys," said the father.

"So did we," said the Leader of the Children.

ENGINE TROUBLE

There were two families with children who had trouble believing in the Tooth Fairy or the Easter Bunny or Santa Claus or goblins or those gnomes who live in the garden and come out at night.

The children in the first family believed only in things that stood up to scrupulous scientific examination.

Their parents tried hard to make them believe in the fanciful notions they enjoyed as children, but found it uphill work.

"How can one rabbit deliver eggs to children all over the world in a night?" asked one child. "Why would a fairy collect teeth?" asked another. "If I see any small people messing around our garden at night, I'll call the police," said another.

A few doors down, in the second family, the parents taught the children not to believe in such things. "The world is much too serious a place for you to be wasting time with that sort of nonsense" they were told time and time again.

One night, on Christmas Eve in fact, the father of the first family drove to his brother's to borrow an old Santa Claus suit. He wanted to surprise his children by delivering a sack of presents as Santa. "I hope they lighten up after this," he told his brother.

As he drove back, however, his car broke down one street from his home. So he got out, slung the sack over his shoulder, and began running up the road.

As he passed the home of the second family, the two children were being told, yet again, what a silly idea Santa Claus was. With heavy hearts they looked out their front window. Santa ran by.

The children yelled in joy at what they had seen, and the parents were lost for an explanation.

When the father got to his own house and triumphantly announced himself as Santa Claus, his children simply reached up and pulled off his beard. Said the youngest child: "What do you think we are? Kids or something?"

GLASS OF WATER

Geraldo stood in the middle of the hot, hot desert with a glass of water in his hand. It was exactly enough to save one life. At his feet lay a person dying of thirst. One hundred metres away lay another person dying of thirst.

Geraldo knelt down to give the person at his feet the glass of water. Then a thought struck him.

"Hang on," he said to himself, pulling the glass of water back from the dying person's scrawny, outstretched arms. "If I save this person, that means I am condemning the other person to death simply because he is far away. I should not discriminate against the other person just because this person is closer to me."

Geraldo then walked over to the other person with his glass of water. By the time he got there, however, the person was dead.

"Oh," said Geraldo.

So he walked back to give the glass of water to the first person. But by the time he returned, that person was also dead.

"Oh," said Geraldo.

The Princess Who Wanted a Life

The beautiful island kingdom of Plushy Knoll was a wonderful place. It was surrounded by crystal waters, blessed with marvellous weather, and had a population of happy, healthy people who kept the local economy well out of debt. And it was run by the most loved royal family there ever was.

They lived in a huge, glittering palace on the top of the highest hill in the kingdom. In the tallest tower of the palace lived a princess who was given everything her heart desired: food, money, jewelry, electronic equipment. Her father and mother had even chosen a husband for her, a handsome prince from another glittering palace just down the road. All seemed right with the fair princess.

"God, I'm bored," said the princess to her father one day. "You say you love me and that the kingdom worships me, but you never let me go out or do anything I want to do."

"That is because we do not want you to do anything that might hurt you," said the wise old king. "And if you read enough magazine sections, you'd know that what young women like doing and what ends up hurting them are usually the same thing."

"But father, I am supposed to be of age," she replied.

"Not while I'm king," said the king, who then locked her in her room and went to work out on his exercise bike.

That night the princess dressed up and ordered a boatman to take her to the country across the water, threatening to have his head chopped off if he said a word. Once there, she hit a few bars and went nightclubbing. She had a great time speaking and dancing with people who had no idea that she was, in fact, a princess.

She met one man she found far more desirable than the beau she had been lined up with. They spent many hours together. As the boatman took the princess back home over the still waters in the early morning, she realised she was in love.

The princess did not feel she had done anything wrong by escaping for the night, but she tossed and turned, guilty that she had deceived her new love.

The next night she went back to the nightclub to meet him. She confessed that she was a person of royal blood whose life was stifled and that she needed a life of her own. Expecting the man to be incensed and insulted, she saw that he only smiled.

"What a coincidence," he said.

THE MEN WHO LET IT RAIN

"Is it my imagination or is it raining like there's no tomorrow?" said Dirk, looking out the window.

"Well, if there is a tomorrow, I'll bet you eight-to-five it'll be a wet one," quipped Kirk, who was also looking out the window.

The office door opened. It was Birk. "Is it raining outside or what?" he said, shaking the rainwater from his hat and trenchcoat, which were drenched.

The three of them fell silent for a while as they gazed at the torrents of water falling from the dark clouds onto the vast city they had built. The rain did not seem to let up.

"Lucky we designed a good drainage system," said Dirk.

"Yep," said Kirk. "And also that we put in extra large catchment areas so at least some of this water won't go to waste."

"And because we put in so many trees and gardens they'll get a good soaking and benefit well from this downpour," said Birk.

Suddenly, Dirk, Kirk and Birk looked at each other, struck with the same idea. Without a word they rushed to their desks and quickly designed cities that could not be touched by rain. Dirk, Kirk and Birk then showed each other their designs.

Dirk's city had a big umbrella over it. Kirk's was designed to float above the clouds. Birk's design, which became their

favorite, was not of a city at all, but of a huge sign to be placed at the city limits. It read:
WELCOME TO OUR LOVELY CITY
Animals, perverts, criminals and rain strictly prohibited.
Fine $200.

They laughed and laughed and laughed. They knew they had great power and talent to build and design and create many things, but they also knew that one thing they could not do was stop the rain.

CyberChrist

The wait for the Messiah had gone on for so long that people began doubting if He would ever come again.

"People are losing faith," said the Leader of the Church to his minions. "We cannot let that happen." They all agreed, and two officers of the Church were charged with finding a solution.

They went to a technological genius and asked her to build a Savior who could do and say all the wonderful things the real one did.

"I can do that," said the technological genius. "But wouldn't people rather wait for the real one?" The Church officers pressed their case and the technological genius shrugged her shoulders. After all, she had a business to run.

She got a brain-dead body and replaced its limbs with powerful artificial ones. She revitalized the brain with a high-performance computer matrix and put a slot in the back of its head where different programs could be set.

The new Messiah was a huge sensation and people quickly came to love Him. He said all the right things, gave blessings and was even able to cure sick people with a touch of His hand. This was nothing divine. A sensor on one finger would diagnose the ailment and a small syringe in another would administer the appropriate cure.

People soon became suspicious of the way the Savior sometimes spoke like a machine, and how there was always a person with a battery pack following Him around, recharging Him and slapping new programs into the back of His head.

"People are starting to see through Him," the officers of the Church said. "We need a miracle to convince them."

"Why don't I feed five thousand people with two fish and five loaves of bread?" said the synthetic Messiah. They thought it was a good idea and tried it, but the Messiah only got through twelve people before He ran out of food.

The people were angry that they had been duped. They captured Him and nailed Him to a cross, knowing full well that He was really a machine. His systems failing, the Messiah turned to heaven and said with a tortured mechanical whine: "Father, forgive them; (beep beep beep) for they know not (whirr whirr) what they do."

The two Church officers watched the spectacle from a distance. "Seems people would rather wait for the real thing," they agreed, which is what the technological genius had said in the first place.

THE ARTIST AND THE EXECUTIVE

An artist came to a film studio with his film, which he considered a great work of art.

"I've got this great movie. It's a masterpiece," said the artist to the executive.

"Really?" said the executive. "What's it called?"

"*From Mountain to Pebble.*"

"Oh? What's it about?"

"The erosion of a mountain."

"Oh really. How long does it run?"

"A little over 2.1 million years."

"Erm..." said the executive.

"Yes?" said the artist.

"Can you cut it a bit?"

"What down to?"

"Say eighty minutes?"

"And compromise my art?"

"Well not compromise, but modify."

"Don't try to sweet-talk me!"

The artist stormed out of the executive's office and left the building with his film, which took four-and-a-half weeks to remove from the waiting room.

THE PHILOSOPHER WHO WAS FULL OF IT

Bobby turned to his friends. "I'm having trouble with life," he said. "I can't sort things out. I need answers." His friends thought this odd, as Bobby had a good job, a good family and what looked like a good life. He seemed to have sorted things out pretty well. But they had some advice for him.

One friend said: "Why don't you just calm down? You're always so tense, worrying over nothing."

Another said: "Go out more. You're always at home. See more movies."

Another said: "Read more. And talk to us. You hardly ever say anything."

But another said: "I've heard of this wise old philosopher who lives far, far away in a distant land who knows all the answers to everything. He might help you."

Bobby decided to seek the philosopher and spent many months travelling great distances to see him. This included swimming an ocean, crossing a desert and scaling a pretty high mountain on top of which the philosopher sat cross-legged, waiting to talk to anyone who had gone to the trouble of coming up to see him.

"Life is simply a series of moments, linked by coincidence," the philosopher told Bobby. "It is a crooked circle that we try to put a line through. Time is an illusion. You give it reality."

There was more. "Love is like a pole: you can get to the top, but only if you climb it. Also it is slippery. And remember that a bubble can burst a thousand times."

Bobby thought to himself for a moment, looked up at the philosopher and said: "What a load of rubbish you talk."

The philosopher shook Bobby's hand, gave him a certificate saying that he had discovered one of the great truths in life, and sent him back to his friends and family.

Bobby had no trouble with life after that.

LITTLE RULES

The Blasting Council from the Intergalactic Committee of Moral Judgment had come to Earth to see if there was any reason why the planet shouldn't be blown into a trillion pieces. As was standard procedure, they randomly selected an inhabitant to explain why the Earth should be spared. This was done out of fairness.

"Why shouldn't we blow you up?" they asked Cheryl, a weedy clerical assistant (third class). She was still a little disoriented, having been kidnapped in her sleep and transported to a huge alien space cruiser in orbit around the Earth.

"Erm, why do you want to blow up the Earth?" she wetly asked of the faceless voices. It was all she could think of. She was still nervous. There was much laughter.

"Because your planet has enough food for everyone, yet most people are starving," said one voice.

"Because you people spend more time hurting each other than helping each other," said another.

"Because you are slowly killing yourselves anyway," said another.

"But we have good in our world," said Cheryl. "We have humanity, we have kindness, we have mercy. We have good intentions and moral endeavors."

"So why is your planet such a mess?" they wanted to know.

"Look," said Cheryl. "I'm not very bright. But there are plenty of people on Earth much smarter than me who can explain this to you much better than I can. They can save the Earth."

They laughed some more. "Don't waste your time thinking about that now," she was told. "You are the one we have chosen. The future of your world is up to you."

"And it doesn't look good," joked one of the council members.

"But why put it on me?" Cheryl asked. They sniggered. "We have this little rule saying that we can choose only one person from each planet to defend itself. And you're it, Sparky."

Cheryl was angry. "But that's a stupid little rule. It's so unfair." They laughed again, more cruelly this time.

"Funny you should say that," said one. "Because our studies show that your world is made up of thousands of little rules, silly ones, which probably explains why your planet is in such a state. So you have one more chance."

Realising she was hamstrung by this little rule, Cheryl tried to make a case for Earth, but she fumbled, bumbled and made a fool of herself. She was sent back to perish with everyone else.

And so it was that the world ended, not with a bang or a whimper, but on a technicality.

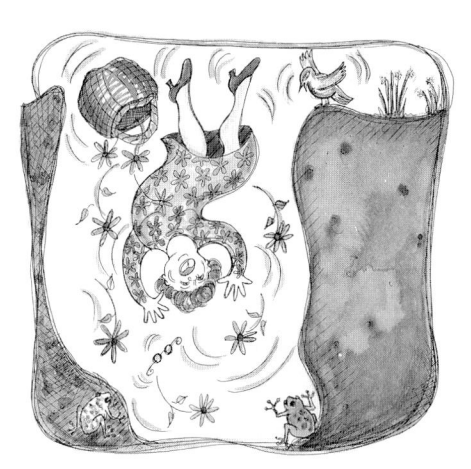

THE WISE OLD WOMAN
WHO WOULDN'T BE TOLD

The wise old woman of the village who knew more than most was walking down the road one fine spring morning, as she always did. She was on her way to the market where each day she would talk and discuss and advise people on the important issues of the day.

As she approached the bridge that she crossed each day, a young man came up to her.

"Excuse me, wise old woman, but you will have to change the way you go to the market this morning. I'm afraid the bridge is out."

"Harrumph," said the sage in disdain. "Are you trying to tell me what to do? Do you know who I am?"

"Yes, of course, but…"

"I will forget more today than you will ever know, young man, and don't you forget that."

"Yes, I'm sure," said the young man, who quickly knelt down, kissed her shoes and got up again. "But the bridge is out, you see, so you can't get to the market without changing your way."

"Bah," said the old woman, and she walked past the young man in a huff.

Then a young woman came up to her and said the same thing.

"Listen," barked the wise old woman. "I don't know what it is with you young people today, trying to tell me my business. I'm older and wiser than you."

"Yes," said the sweet young girl. "Of course you are, I realise that and I don't mean any disrespect, but, you see, well, the thing is that the bridge is out, and you can't go the way you usually go."

"Go away," said the wise old woman, who continued down the road.

As she got closer and closer to the bridge, many more people from the village pleaded with her to change her route, but she brushed them all aside. Even large signs that said "BRIDGE OUT! PLEASE TURN BACK" did not dissuade her from her course.

And so it was that the wise old woman continued on down the road she always took and defiantly took the bridge that wasn't there. She fell into the deep ravine and was killed instantly. It was in all the papers.

TERRORIST OF LOVE

A man in love wanted to hear from the woman he loved that she loved him. All he wanted was a sign. So he put one bullet in a revolver, spun the chambers and held the gun to the back of the woman's head.

"There is one bullet in this gun," he said lovingly. "Now, either I can pull the trigger or you can give me a kiss. The choice is yours."

The woman didn't need any time to think about what she was going to say.

"Pull the trigger," she said. "I'd rather take my chances than the choice you've given me."

Then man's hard face melted with sadness. "Really?" he mourned, as the hand with the gun dropped to his side. "Yes," she said.

Then he put the gun into his own mouth. It was a ploy to get sympathy.

"Now you have a choice," the woman said. "You can either pull the trigger or allow me the freedom to choose whether I want you or not."

He thought a moment. The thrill of being chosen would have been big, but the fear of rejection was bigger. So he pulled the trigger, and left quite a mess on the wall.

PHIL JUNIOR OF FLYLAND

Deep in the forest, past the creek, over the hill and left at the big oak was a clearing where lived a colony of flies. Well, not a colony, really, more just a bunch of flies who happened to live in roughly the same place.

As far as flies went they did not have much to tell them apart: they all flew, they all made buzzing sounds when they flew, and they were all flies. They were also a favourite delicacy for spiders, who knew the place where the flies lived very well, and set up webs around the place to catch them.

Fortunately, one fly, Phil junior, was wise to the spiders' schemes, and did not want to see his fellow flies get eaten.

"Watch out for spider webs," Phil junior would say.

The flies he told this to were not blessed with above-average intelligence, otherwise they would have moved on away from the spiders. But they sure knew good advice when they heard it.

"Thank you," they would tell Phil.

Sometimes when Phil junior gave his advice to the older flies, they would thank him and say "Just like your father, you are. Always ready with a kind and helpful word."

One morning, however, tragedy struck. Phil junior was

found dead – caught in a spider's web. All the flies who knew Phil gathered around and watched helplessly as the spider leisurely tucked into Phil.

"What an unfortunate way for Phil junior to go," said one fly.

"Never hurt a soul," said another.

"To be caught in the type of trap you spent all of your life warning others about is such a shame," said another.

"And it's funny," mourned one of the elders. "That's how his father went, too."

MODERN FRIENDS

John and Jake met on the first day of kindergarten and were friends from then on.

They did everything together. They played together, they worked together, they ate together. At high school they studied together, dated together, failed subjects together and, occasionally, even cheated together.

They went to university together and graduated together. They were happy together at the ceremony but were tearful afterwards because they feared that going out into the rat race of the job market would separate them.

Kind fate, however, saw to it that John and Jake landed jobs in the same company. To their immense joy, they worked not only for the same people, but in the same building, and on the same floor.

For the first six months, John and Jake worked hard to please their employers, who rewarded them with pay rises, promotions and cellular phones.

John and Jake had lunch every day, basking in each other's success and happiness, still high on the idea that having been through so many of life's highs and lows together, they were still together.

Soon, though, they began cancelling on each other, for this reason, for that reason. Whether at work, before work or after work, they never quite had time for each other. But there was always an excuse and an apology and a promise to make it up.

"We must catch up soon," each told the other in turn.

The time between engagements stretched from weeks to months to years, until finally they did get together for lunch.

"It's been a long time," said John.

"Sure has," said Jake. "We have a lot to catch up on."

But each time one of them started to say something, a cellular phone would ring, or a fax would arrive, or there would be a call on the restaurant phone or a business associate would walk by that they just had to have a few words with.

Before they knew it, lunch was over. "We must do this again soon," they promised each other.

John and Jake worked on the same floor of the same building for the rest of their lives, but they never did catch up after that.

Seven Short Naked Men

The rumor was rife among the members of the tribe of Short Naked Men that the view over the wall was sensational, and Gavin was more keen than anyone to see the view.

He had many reasons for this, not the least of which was his belief that the view would reveal a tribe of Tall Naked Women.

But because the wall was so tall Gavin knew that the only way he could get a glimpse of the view was to stand atop six other Short Naked Men, standing on each other's shoulders.

He had trouble getting the support he needed, but eventually convinced six other Short Naked Men to take part in his scheme. The only way he could do this, however, was if he promised to be at the bottom of the column of Short Naked Men, supporting everyone else.

This was not what Gavin originally had in mind, but he figured this way he would get at least some idea of what the view was like.

"When you see the view," Gavin said to the Short Naked Man who was to be on top, "be sure to pass it down to the next person so he can pass it on down until the details get to me."

So the seven Short Naked Men stood one on top of the other, with Gavin at the bottom straining under the weight.

Gavin sent a message up the column to the top man, the first member of the tribe of Short Naked Men to ever peer over the wall. "Is the view wonderful?" he wanted to know.

It was magnificent. Rolling hills, glistening streams, unicorns, butterflies, flowers, green fields and, yes, a tribe of beautiful Tall Naked Women.

The man on top, having feasted his eyes on the glorious view, passed the description down to the next man, who passed it on down to the man below him and so on until the details dribbled down to the man standing on Gavin's shoulders.

"What's it like? What's it like?" Gavin asked excitedly.

"Nothing much, apparently," he told Gavin. "Just a hill and some water."

THE BEAST AND THE LEASH

Young Tad went shopping with his mother one day, down to the big mall on the outskirts of their brand new suburb. There he saw in the window of a pet shop a little baby beast that looked at him in such a way that he knew it was just for him.

"Mummy, Mummy," Tad yelled out. "Buy me the beast! Buy me the beast!"

"I'll buy you the beast," said Tad's mother. "But you have to love it and care for it and clean up after it."

"Oh I will," said Tad. "Just get me the damn thing."

And so Tad's mother bought him the beast, and to her great surprise Tad was true to his word. He washed the beast and fed it and even cleaned up after it, although this was something he did not do with great enthusiasm.

The beast, in return, loved and cherished Tad. It was also very loving to all the people it met, even strangers. It loved to play games and run after sticks, catching balls in its mouth and occasionally upturning old car wrecks.

Soon, though, Tad saw that the beast began to grow a little too large and seemed to be a bit too boisterous for his liking.

"Hmm, time I put a leash on this thing before it gets out of control," said Tad, who was also growing up.

The beast was not too keen about the leash, and

protested with howls and whines as Tad clasped the collar around its neck.

With the leash Tad could pretty much control the beast. He could make it sit, stand, walk and run around in circles. One thing he could not control, however, was the anger of the beast, which began biting Tad at every opportunity in rebellion against its leash.

But each time the beast bit Tad, it reinforced in Tad's mind that the leash should remain.

This went on for about a year.

"Have you thought about maybe letting the beast off the leash?" asked Tad's mother as she tended to his thousandth bite wound with a bottle of disinfectant and a bandage.

He thought it was a stupid idea, but he gave it a shot and removed the leash. To his astonishment, the beast began behaving exactly as it had before the leash was put on, and was as loving and as sweet and as obedient as ever.

Tad discovered by letting the beast off the leash that he didn't need one. His mother watched from the doorway as Tad and beast played in the back yard as they had before, and marvelled that her son had just grown up some more.

Mrs Octopus Gets Down to Business

Mrs Octopus was not in a good mood. "And so why are you late tonight, bright boy?" she asked.

"I was working late at the office," said Mr Octopus as he slithered through the front door and over to the fridge to get a can of plankton.

"Oh, really? And so why didn't you call me to say you'd be this late?" she wanted to know.

"Didn't I call you?"

"No, you didn't. Why not?"

"I must have been too busy."

"When *I'm* working late at the office I always manage to call you," she said.

Mrs Octopus had a point.

"I think you're lying to me," Mrs Octopus went on. "I think you were at the pub with those stupid friends of yours playing darts and arm-wrestling."

She had a point there, too, because it was true.

"Look, sweetheart, I can prove to you that I'm not lying," said Mr Octopus. He pulled a piece of paper from one of his eight trouser pockets and gave it to her. It was a signed note from all the people he worked with saying that he was, in fact, late because he had worked back at the office.

Mr Octopus then gave Mrs Octopus a stone tablet on which his reason for being late was engraved.

54

He then took her outside, where a large sign painted on the side of the hull of a sunken ocean liner read: "I was late because I worked back at the office."

But no matter how much Mr Octopus tried, he could not change the fact that Mrs Octopus could see in his beady little eyes that if he had had any teeth, he would have been lying through them.

This was not the first time Mr Octopus had tried this trick on Mrs Octopus, either. And she was fed up.

So she kicked him in the tentacles.

THE HUG OF DOOM

For a long time little Bobby Balloon had wanted to play with little Peter Prickle, who lived just across the street. But his mother, a large and wise balloon who knew the ways of the world, would brook no argument.

"You will never play with little Peter Prickle," she would tell Bobby as he floated around, trying to nag permission out of her.

"But why, oh why?" he would ask.

"For reasons that are too horrid to contemplate," she would say, and that would be the end of the matter.

Little Peter Prickle also wanted to play with little Bobby Balloon, but his mother, a strong and excessively sharp prickle who had been around the block a few times, would not allow it.

"Why ever not?" little Peter Prickle would ask.

"Because if you two ever got close something dreadful would happen and you'd never forgive yourself, or forgive me for allowing you." And that would be the end of the matter.

Peter and Bobby had asked their mothers many times for details about what it was that would happen that was so awful if they ever became friends, but each time they were simply and sternly told to shut up, do as they were told and to never ever play with each other.

But curiosity eventually got the better of Peter and

Bobby. They arranged a secret meeting so they could play and see how things went.

They had a great time. They played football and cricket and wrestled a bit. They made sandcastles and ran and even read some books together.

"I think we've been fed a lot of hooey," said Bobby Balloon.

"Me too," said Peter Prickle. And so they became secret friends, meeting and playing when they could without anyone knowing.

Soon, though, the mothers twigged to what was going on and caught them in the act of enjoying each other's company.

"What are you two doing?" asked Mother Prickle.

"If Bobby touches Peter he will explode!" said Mother Balloon.

"But we have touched many times and no such thing has ever happened," they said, laughing. To demonstrate they hugged. Bobby detonated into a thousand pieces. The shock killed Peter.

"Kids these days. I dunno," said Mother Prickle.

"You said a mouthful," said Mother Balloon. "If only they'd learn to listen."

THE DIAMOND KEYRING THAT WENT FOR A SWIM

Mack could not believe his luck, so he told George. "You know that gorgeous woman I met at the casino last night?"

"You mean the one wearing the diamond necklace and the diamond earrings and that diamond-studded dress with the diamond brooch, who bought you all those drinks and kept calling you 'Mr Wonderful'?"

"The same. Guess what? I just got a package from her. Look!" Mack showed George the little box he had just received. In it was a golden house-key that glistened and sparkled in the mid-afternoon sun. It was attached to a custom-designed, fully addressed keyring studded with the most expensive diamonds, which also glistened and sparkled.

"What do you think?" said Mack.

"I'm taking a royal stab in the dark here, but I think she likes you. You going over?"

"Soon as next shift arrives," said Mack, who put the diamond keyring into his top shirt pocket. He then bent down to tie his shoelace, which had come loose in all the excitement. As he did, however, the diamond keyring fell out of his pocket.

If his luck had held out a second longer, Mack would simply have picked it up and put it back in his pocket.

Unfortunately, however, Mack and George worked in a toxic waste treatment plant, and the diamond keyring had the great misfortune to fall into a drum of horrid, sludgy muck that stank to high heaven and looked just awful.

"Bugger!" said Mack.

"What are you gonna do?" asked George.

"What do you think?" said Mack as he rolled up his sleeve and, with the greatest reluctance, reached into the drum of horrible smelly waste to fish out the diamond keyring. It took some minutes, but eventually he found it.

"Well, that has certainly taught you a valuable lesson," said George.

"Sure has," said Mack. "Sometimes you have to go through things that are awful and terrible to get to something good."

"Yeeeeah, that too," George said slowly. "I was actually thinking more about the wisdom of not putting diamond keyrings in your top pocket. They fall out otherwise. Also, you should bend at the knees more."

Jasper's Big Trip

Jasper always liked to be sure of everything. He was sure he was a happy person. He was sure he was respected the world over.

He was sure he was the second best scientist in the world.

And he was sure he would have been the *best* scientist in the world, if it weren't for that bitch Robinson.

Robinson worked in the lab across the road, and as much as Jasper tried, he was never able to invent anything quite as brilliant as Robinson did.

Each time Jasper came up with something fantastic – a milk carton opener, a battery that never ran flat, a voice-operated VCR timer – the response from his peers and the press was always the same: "Wow, Jasper, that's fantastic! But you know what? Robinson invented something just last week that's even better!"

Having tolerated this for many years, Jasper decided it was high time he secured himself as Number One by taking care of Robinson once and for all.

Of course, killing or maiming her was out of the question because it would cause too much trouble.

Instead, Jasper decided to travel back in time, to the day Robinson's parents were married. He would arrive just before they took their vows and prevent the marriage by killing one of them.

"I'll be just like whatsisname in that movie," Jasper thought as he drew up the blueprints for his time machine.

Some months of hard work later he was ready to go. The only snag was that time travel was such a strain on the molecules it was only possible for him to ever take one round trip through time. Anything more, Jasper calculated, would result in his complete disintegration, with his molecules being sprinkled across the expanse of the space–time continuum.

Jasper sat in the time machine, punched in the time, date, year and location of the wedding of Robinson's parents and sent himself back. He arrived an instant later in the forecourt of the church. The place was deserted, but for the priest who was sweeping up the streamers and confetti that covered the ground.

"Aren't the Robinsons getting married here today?" asked Jasper.

"They did get married here today," said the priest. "One hour ago."

Jasper had forgotten about daylight saving. Robinson would be born after all. Now Jasper had to travel back to his own time and live with it.

THE LOLLIPOP ANGEL

No matter what the people of Dapper Valley did, no matter how hard they worked or how long they prayed, they just couldn't get it right. Their crops failed, their plumbing creaked and their centralized transit system just never seemed to click.

One particularly famished summer's day, an angel appeared to all the people of this sad little community.

"What are you, a messenger from God here to tell us how screwed we are?" one person said.

"No," the angel said. "I have not come to judge you. I am the Lollipop Angel. I have come to bring you happiness."

"And how are you going to do that?" the townsfolk asked. The angel then began handing out lollipops to each and every citizen of Dapper Valley.

"These will make you happy and hopefully inspire you to greater things," the Angel said.

Indeed, the lollipops did bring happiness to the people of Dapper Valley, but not quite the kind of happiness the Lollipop Angel had in mind. The people now seemed happy to put up with all the things that had made their life such a misery as long as they had enough lollipops to suck on. They enjoyed this new view of life so much they didn't want the angel to leave.

"Give us more," they said.

"Are you sure?" the Lollipop Angel said.

"Hey," someone said. "You said you weren't here to judge us, so shut up and make with the lollipops."

Being true to her word, the Lollipop Angel obliged until the people of Dapper Valley had stockpiled enough lollipops to last a century.

"The time has come for me to go," the Lollipop Angel told the townsfolk as they sucked and slurped away on their bounty. "But are you sure you are happy?"

"Yes," they said. "Come back soon, but next time remember to bring more strawberry."

And so the people of Dapper Valley enjoyed their lollipops as a sign that at least one thing in their rotten and horrid world had gone right for them.

Two years later another angel arrived. "Who are you?" they asked.

"I'm the Dental Hygiene Angel," she said as she set up her drill. "Who's first?"

The line that formed was very long.

REVALUING THE CONTENTS OF ROBBIE'S HEAD

There was trouble at the palace. The empire had been going well under the old king, but a member of the king's court thought he would make a better king, so he got some friends together, sneaked up behind the old king and cut his head off.

"I'm the new king now," said the new king to the old king's court. "And a new king means new rules. And rule number one is, get rid of the old king's court."

Before anyone could protest, the members of the old king's court had their heads cut off. This was not a great idea, especially when it came to chopping off the head of Robbie, a clerk who, despite his lowly position, knew everything about running the empire. Everyone knew this, too – even those who helped the new king in his coup. They all said how useful it would be to not cut off Robbie's head. But the new king said "Cut his head off," so they cut his head off.

Having "flushed out the old guard", as the new king liked to put it, the new court tried to get things going again. But nothing worked because nobody knew anything. The only person who did was Robbie, and he had just had his head cut off. So the new king called a meeting.

"Seems as though we need Robbie more alive than dead," said the king. "I hereby decree that Robbie be reinstated immediately."

The king's court looked a little perplexed at this announcement, but they did what the king said. He was, after all, the king.

They went to the graveyard where Robbie had been buried, dug up his grave, opened the coffin and there he was, rotting, being eaten by worms, with his head clearly detached from the rest of his body.

"OK you guys," said the king, "get him out of there and back to work."

"But sire," said one of the king's minions, shaking with fear, "we can't."

"Why not?!" demanded the king.

"Because you cut his head off."

"Listen," said the king, his cheeks bright red with fury. "If you lot can't do it, I'll chop off all your heads and get some guys who can."

They immediately took Robbie back to the palace, where they taped his head to his body, cleaned him up, dressed him in the uniform of the court and sat him at his old desk.

The king visited him the next day. "First day back on the job, eh Robbie?" said the king. "How's it feel, buddy?" The king slapped Robbie on the back as a friendly gesture of encouragement and support. Robbie's head rolled off and hit the floor with a clunk.

E D D I E   A N D   T H E   C A N Y O N

The first Eddie heard about how worthless he was, was the memo he got from his boss.
MEMO TO: EDDIE
FROM: THE BOSS

Eddie,
You are a worthless schlub.
Clear your desk and get out.
(PS: thank you for the 25 years' service.)

So Eddie, being the loyal employee that he was, promptly cleared his desk and left quietly, not wanting to cause the company any trouble.

"At least I have a wife who loves me," said Eddie, as the security guard gave him a kick in the bum for luck.

When he got home, however, he found a note from his wife stuck to the fridge door by a small plastic pineapple.

"You're a worthless schlub, Eddie," said the note. "I've left you. And I've taken the VCR."

"At least I have a dog who loves me," said Eddie. But when he went out to feed it, the dog was nowhere to be found. On the dog's kennel was taped a small note. "I've taken the dog, too," it read.

"At least I have a goldfish who loves me," said Eddie. But when he went to feed it, he found another note taped to the side of the tank. "And the goldfish," it read.

Eddie felt down, so he went to the doctor. This is what he was told. "There is nothing I can do for you. You are a worthless schlub, Eddie, and it might be terminal." He turned to his family, but they said he was a worthless schlub too.

At every job Eddie went for, the inevitable response he got was "Why should we hire you? Everybody says what a totally worthless schlub you are." Eddie felt so insignificant even automatic doors refused to open for him. He would ask them why. They would tell him it was because he was worthless, and to take the side door.

Eddie decided to jump off a cliff. Just before the big moment he yelled out into the canyon. "I AM a worthwhile human being!" A few seconds later an echo answered. "No you're not, Eddie. You're a worthless schlub."

Eddie thought he was imagining things, so he tried again.

"I AM a worthwhile human being!" he yelled.

"No you're not, cheeseface. You're worthless," said the echo.

"Am not," said Eddie.

"Are too," said the echo.

"Listen," said Eddie. "I don't care what you say, or what anyone else says any more. I'm not jumping off this cliff and you can stick your opinion up your canyon."

Eddie waited a few seconds for the reply.

"That's more like it," said the echo.

From then on whatever trials Eddie faced (and there were many) he was fortified by the knowledge that there was at least one person on his side – one person, and one very special echo.

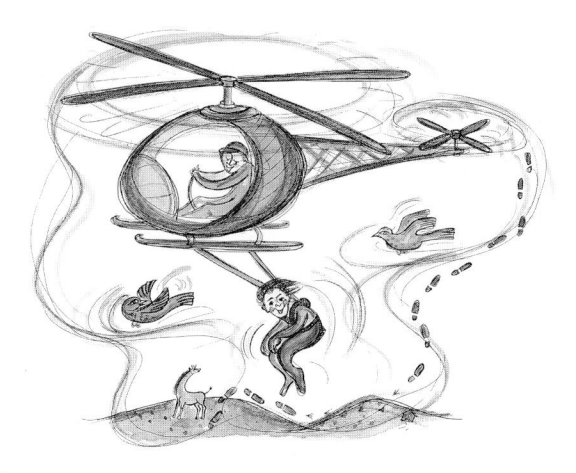

UPRIGHT AND UPTIGHT IN THE LAND OF NOD

Nobody in the land of Nod could walk as well as Wanda. This was because nobody else in the land of Nod could walk at all.

Wanda could walk to any place she wanted to. She would walk to this place and that place, to any place at all.

Everyone else had to be transported by cranes, cars, specially designed trains, helicopters and wheelchairs. The wheelchairs either were motorized or had to be pushed along by people who were in wheelchairs that were motorized.

There was nothing wrong with everyone else's legs. They were perfectly healthy. They just could not figure out how Wanda did it.

"How do you do it, Wanda?" they would ask.

"I don't know," she would say. "It just comes naturally."

One day Wanda was pressed on the subject by Winnie, a close friend. "Come on Wan," she said in a desperate whisper. "I'm sick to death of having to be moved about like a lump of meat. Tell me how you do it."

Because Winnie was a close friend, Wanda tried to explain how she walked.

"Well, what I do is stand up, then I move my left leg forward, while keeping my right leg rigid. Then I move my right leg forward and then... no wait, it's my right leg first and then my left, and then my right, and then... no, hang on, it's my left first, then right, then..."

Before she knew it, Wanda collapsed to the ground. She tried getting up, thinking about which leg to move first, but she just couldn't get the sequence right.

Wanda spent the rest of her life having to move around in a wheelchair, travelling to this place and that by helicopters and cars and trains and cranes.

"I'm sorry I caused you all this trouble," said Winnie, who was still her close friend.

"That's OK," said Wanda. "I can't blame you for asking. I can only blame myself for answering."

THE LIFE OF THE LINGS

One very small moment, on a very small day, in a business that liked to think it was very big, but which was actually very small, one very small person said something they shouldn't have to another very small person.

The reason they shouldn't have was that the person who had said the thing was slightly smaller than the person he had said it to. An Underling had spoken to an Upperling in a way that Underlings were not allowed to.

"Doesn't that Underling know who I am?" said the Upperling to the Middling.

"Obviously not," said the Middling, "otherwise he would not have spoken that way."

"I want that Underling punished severely," said the Upperling.

"You want him fired?" asked the Middling.

"No, no. We need the manpower. Besides, I don't really have the authority. Just scare him. Make him think that he might be fired. Make him sweat for a couple of days. Go forth and put the fear of God into him."

"The fear of God?" asked the Middling.

"Just do it and stop questioning my authority, or you'll be in trouble, too. Remember…"

"I know, sir. I'm just a Middling."

So the Middling went to the Underling and told him that the person he had said the thing to was an Upperling. The Underling was shocked and said he'd never have said a thing if he had known. He also said he was sorry.

Sorry wasn't enough, said the Middling. But rather than tell him his job was on the line, the Middling instead told the Underling that the Upperling only wanted him to think that he might lose his job, just to scare him.

"So what should I do?" asked the Underling.

"Just act scared for a couple of days, and from now on watch what you say and who you say it to."

This the Underling did, and even though nobody had done what they were supposed to, everybody got what they wanted: the Upperling was made to feel important; the Underling got to keep his job without having to be humiliated; and the Middling, as usual, quietly rejoiced that he had once again kept the world from destroying itself.

The Woodpecker and the Tree

There once was a woodpecker who lived in a tree with one branch. The woodpecker liked the tree a lot because it had only one branch, which meant that the woodpecker had the tree all to itself.

The tree liked the woodpecker a lot, too. "If I had a whole lot of branches you are still the only bird I would allow to sit on me," said the tree to the woodpecker. "That's nice," said the woodpecker.

After some time, the woodpecker decided it was time to spread its wings and fly off for a while. The tree was deeply distressed at this, and asked the woodpecker if it would stay on the branch and not go.

"I must go and see more of the world," said the woodpecker, as kindly as it could.

"But I am so used to having you here, how will I cope? And what if you never come back? I don't want you to go. Please don't."

So the woodpecker flew off to a nearby shopping mall and returned with a T-shirt in its beak to show the tree. It read:

> *If you love something set it free.*
> *If it comes back, it's yours.*
> *If it doesn't, it never was...*

The words were accompanied by a nice picture of a seagull on a beach.

"What the hell does that mean?" said the tree.

"It means I'm going, but that I know what my leaving means to you." With that the woodpecker flew off to see the world.

Some years later the woodpecker, having tasted the world, felt a longing for the tree who had been its friend for so long, and decided to return to it. It looked forward to seeing the tree again and to the warm reception the tree would no doubt extend once it saw that the woodpecker had, in fact, come back.

When the woodpecker returned, however, there was no sign of the tree. It had not been cut down. It had simply moved on, root system and all.

The woodpecker did not understand this at all and went back to the shopping mall to see if it had somehow misread the message on the T-shirt it had shown the tree all those years before. The words on the front were the same:

If you love something set it free.

If it comes back, it's yours.

If it doesn't, it never was...

On the back, however, were more. They read:

...but that doesn't mean you have to wait around.

The words were accompanied by a nice picture of a tree with one branch with a bird on it. The bird was not a woodpecker.

DRAGON FRIEND

Martha was scared out of her wits, but she dared not scream or yell or make any noise at all, lest she startle the dragon that her husband, Morrie, was cautiously trying to feed.

No dragon had ever touched down in the castle grounds before. The closest Martha or Morrie ever got to them was at dusk each night as they watched the dragons fly overhead in huge, orderly squadrons to their traditional feeding grounds much further south.

Yet now a dragon had perched upon a small outcrop of rock very near the castle gates, looking curiously at the offering of bread Morrie held out in his hand as he tried to befriend this magnificent beast.

Slowly, as if understanding the amity of the gesture, the dragon outstretched a spidery talon. Strong enough to crush a boulder, the claw delicately pinched the food scrap and placed it in the dragon's mouth.

On a knife-edge of fear and curiosity, Martha came up alongside her husband and offered the dragon a cup of water and a small piece of meat, which it accepted with the same uncharacteristic repose.

Martha and Morrie stood before the dragon, totally at its mercy should it decide, at a whim, to crush them with its claws, kill them with a lethal bite or incinerate them with one blast of its fiery breath. But it did not. After a few more feedings, it flew off and joined the flock.

Each night, for weeks afterwards, the same dragon descended from the skies to partake of Martha and Morrie's hospitality while its brethren continued south. This it did with more and more familiarity until it became almost a house pet.

Martha and Morrie came to love the dragon, and even named it. They fed it nicer and nicer titbits, and the dragon responded in kind by protecting their land and gracing the grounds with its magnificent presence.

Much as they loved the dragon, they held to one hard and fast rule: "Don't ever, ever, let the dragon in the house." They were pretty good at abiding by this, but one afternoon, during some spring cleaning, they left a large window open to air out the rooms in one of the towers.

The dragon seized the opportunity to enter Martha and Morrie's castle, pluck their two children from their cribs, and fly off again into the sky, never to return.

The Tale of Spiteful Brett

Someone had done Brett wrong, so he was going to do them wrong. But Brett did not just want to do them wrong once. He wanted to do them wrong again and again and again.

"Enough with the revenge!" screamed his victim. "I get your point. I'm sorry I did you wrong."

"Not as sorry as you're going to be," said Brett, who kept his torture up for months and years. He became quite good at it, so everyone who crossed Brett got the same treatment.

"Don't you think you've given those poor wretches enough of their own medicine?" asked a friend, who was getting worried about Brett's state of mind.

"Not nearly enough," said Brett.

"When will it be enough, Brett?" the concerned friend asked.

"When they lie dead and buried and stinking in the earth," said Brett, who gave out a maniacal laugh as he plotted to make things even worse for his enemies.

Brett's friend told another of his friends, and together they managed to wrest Brett away from his scheme for just a few moments so he could get a good look at it from a sobering distance.

"Can you see what you're doing?" said one of the friends.

"Oh my God, did I do that?" asked Brett, horrified.

"Don't speak in the past tense," said the friend. "You are still doing it."

Brett agreed to see a doctor, as he had had no idea he had gone so far. The doctor came back with a disturbing diagnosis.

"Am I mad for doing all these things?" asked Brett nervously.

"No, you're not mad, you're something far worse," said the doctor. "You're normal."

SQUIRKY GETS READY

As rare and difficult as it was for squirrels to be exceptional in any way at all, Squirky was, nonetheless, an exceptional squirrel.

All the other squirrels in the woods stored enough nuts to get them through winter, but most of the time they just lived on whatever nuts they came across from day to day.

Squirky, however, had a huge storehouse of nuts he was always adding to, for Squirky had a theory, a theory about the future.

"You must save for the future, plan for the future, prepare for the future," he would say to his fellow squirrels. "What if there's another ice age, or a flood, or some toxic cloud that drifts over from the city and renders all the nut-bearing trees barren? What will you all do then?"

"Steal from you," they joked.

"No way," he would answer. "I have my eyes on the future, always on the future."

Squirky was admired for his forward thinking, but it did make him a drag when it came to afternoon coffee at his place.

"How about a few nuts with the coffee, Squirky?" his friends would ask.

"No way, I'm saving them for the future," he would say, offering them a digestive biscuit instead.

"So you have your nuts, but what are your plans for the future?" they would ask.

"To be ready for it," Squirky would say. It was as specific as he ever got.

This made his friends crazy, and drove female squirrels away, even those who wanted to share the future with him.

Eventually all the squirrels grew very old, with barely enough eyesight left to keep them from bumping into trees and falling off branches.

One by one they died off until Squirky was alone, with nothing but his nuts, no future, and a life made empty by the fallacy that the future is something you wait for.

VAL AND VIN GO FOR A SPIN

Val and Vin had been flying a long time and thought they knew everything about airplanes. But they didn't know what was going on when their airplane suddenly spun out of control and began tumbling towards the earth.

They tried everything to regain control, but it was no use. Reason quickly gave way to panic.

"I think we're going to die," screamed Val.

"Certainly looks like it," screamed Vin. "Unless we get lucky."

"I don't believe in luck," said Val. "Only God can save us now."

"I don't believe in God," said Vin. "Only luck can save us."

Just as their lives began flashing before them and things looked hopeless, the plane magically slowed down, levelled out and drifted gently to the ground. Many experts tried to explain Val and Vin's miraculous escape from certain death with weather charts and diagrams of how odd aerodynamics can sometimes be, but Val and Vin had their own beliefs.

"It was God," said Val.

"It was luck," said Vin.

Val and Vin then took a long boat cruise together. In the middle of the sea the ship hit a rock and sank. Val and Vin were the only two survivors.

"It was God," said Val.
"It was luck," said Vin.

While driving a car one day, they lost a front wheel and careened into a stream of oncoming traffic. Many people died, but Val and Vin did not get so much as a scratch.

"It was God," said Val.
"It was luck," said Vin.

One night soon after, Val and Vin died in their sleep. The next thing they knew they were floating among clouds populated by angels. Everything was wonderful. They were in Heaven.

"Now I believe in God," said Vin.
"Now I believe in luck," said Val.

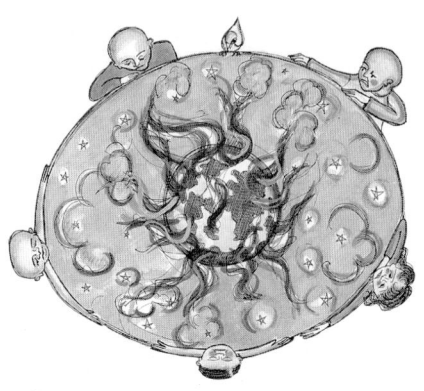

PLANET HOPE

The time had come for the world to end, not with a whimper, but with the loudest of bangs.

For days, the population of the planet had gathered in orderly groups at various launch sites, where they waited patiently to board the huge interstellar spaceships that would take them to their new home, far from the doomed planet that had been theirs for thousands of generations.

For weeks, everyone – from the lowliest workers to the exalted members of the World Council – had prepared for the departure, packing their most precious belongings, farewelling the homes and landscapes that had become part of their lives, trying to adjust to the idea of life on a new world.

For months, the ships had been designed and built to make sure that every single member of the united civilization that had graced the planet for so many millennia would have a seat, as well as room enough for at least some of their possessions.

For centuries everyone knew this was going to happen, that their world would end, not because of abuse, for they had cared for it so, but because there was only so long it could remain before collapsing in on itself and exploding into stardust.

For years and years they tried working out ways to prevent this. They called upon every resource they had and took direction from the most brilliant minds, minds produced by a united world culture devoted to intellect, harmony, progress and technology; this culture had cured all diseases, made uninhabitable worlds livable, built the most magnificent structures and bestowed upon every citizen a life span many, many times that given to them by nature.

They tried to figure out formulas to strengthen the crust of the planet, to cool its core, to temper the increasingly wild climate as the planet became less and less stable, but nothing worked.

The scientists, technicians, engineers and advisers who had devoted themselves to this venture for centuries were the last people left on the planet. But as the winds got stronger, the air got hotter and the ground began to buckle under their feet, they too boarded their rocketship and fled.

They joined the others in orbit, despairing and accepting with them that, for all their technology and wisdom, all they could do was retreat to a safe distance and watch.

The Old Man at the Lights

For as long as anyone could remember, the old man at the lights had always been there, standing at the corner, watching the traffic lights but never crossing the road. He was thought odd, but as he bothered nobody, took up very little room and was very quiet he was left to himself.

Samuel had grown up knowing about the old man at the lights, but it was not until he was fully grown that he began to get curious.

Each morning, Samuel would watch the old man staring blankly at the lights. Out of politeness Samuel would say nothing, but one day his curiosity overwhelmed his manners.

"Excuse me, old man," Samuel said. "What are you doing, exactly?"

"I'm waiting for the lights to change," said the old man.

This seemed a strange thing to say, thought Samuel, as the lights changed regularly every few minutes. Samuel tried explaining this to the old man, but all the old man ever said was: "I'm waiting for the lights to change."

Thinking the old man a fool, Samuel made a habit of ridiculing him each morning, to which the old man's only reply was: "I'm waiting for the lights to change." Samuel even took friends down to see the old man at the lights. Samuel was a little ashamed of this, until he discovered that everyone else was doing exactly the same thing, and for exactly the same reasons.

Then, one day, the old man at the lights was not there. Nobody knew what had happened to him. He simply vanished. All that was left of him were two little bald patches in the grass next to the pole where the old man's feet had been.

Instinctively, Samuel stood in the footprints, and his life changed.

His normal perception of reality gave way to a staggering, paradimensional cognition where the space–time continuum melted, allowing Samuel to travel from one end of the cosmos to the other in the blink of an eye, to visit any moment in history or the future, to meet anyone he wished, to make love to all the women he had ever desired.

Somewhere, on the distant periphery of his consciousness, Samuel was vaguely aware of people asking him things. He did not know what they said, and he did not know what he said in reply.

Nor did he care, for Samuel now enjoyed life in a manner that was utterly beyond the experience and imagination of every single other creature in all of creation – every single other creature, that is, except one.

A DAY AT THE ZOO

One fine day at the zoo a little child asked her father a question about a creature in one of the enclosures.

"Daddy?"

"Yes, my child."

"Why does the giraffe have such a long neck?"

"So it can reach the leaves at the top of the tree."

"Did it always have a long neck?"

"No, it once had a short neck, but after a million years it grew a long neck so it could feed on the leaves no other animal could reach."

In front of another enclosure the child had another question.

"Daddy?"

"Yes, my child."

"Why are the ostriches so tall and skinny?"

"So they can quickly run away from animals trying to eat them."

"Were they always tall and skinny?"

"No, they were once short and fat, but after a million years they became tall and skinny so they could run from danger."

In front of another enclosure the child had another question.

"Daddy?"

"Yes, my child."

"Why does the camel have a hump on its back?"

"So it can store food and water for a long, long time without having to eat or drink."

"Did it always have a hump?"

"No. It used to have a flat back, but after a million years it grew one so it could survive."

Inside one enclosure were two people yelling at each other.

"What's this, Daddy?" asked the child.

"This is two people trying to get along."

"What have *they* developed over the last million years to help them get along?" the child asked.

"I don't know," said the father.

"Do they love each other?"

"I don't know."

"Do they hate each other?"

"I don't know."

"Do they know each other?"

"I don't know."

"How long have they been at it?"

"About a million years."

"Will they be better in another million years?"

"I don't know," said the father. "We'll have to come back in a million years and see."

"So long as they can survive the next five minutes," said the child.

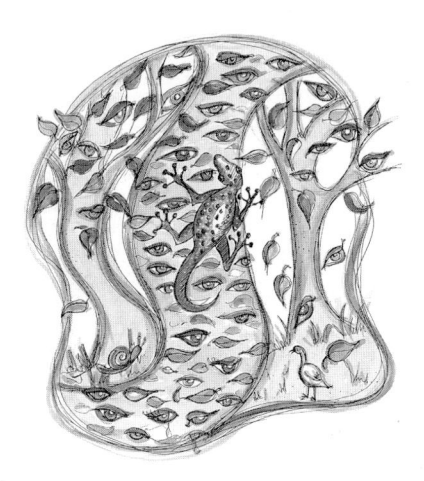

THE CUTE, FURRY POSSUM TWINS

The cute, furry possum twins were walking down the track one day, through the most beautiful part of the forest where they had lived for many years.

The twins had been straight for quite some time, although they felt very strongly that their standing in the forest community was still sullied by their careers in petty crime, which included convictions for stealing, vandalism and ringbarking without a licence.

Luckily, they kept out of jail on the proviso that they behaved. This the possum twins agreed to, though they didn't feel they were liked much, especially the elder twin, who was thirty-seven seconds older.

As they walked, they noticed a lizard strolling towards them. When they passed each other, the lizard gave the possum twins a small smile. The possum twins smiled back, and continued on their way as the lizard continued on his.

"I bet he means that," said the elder possum sarcastically.

"What do you mean?" asked the younger.

"He probably thinks what low-life scum we are and that we should be in jail. It gets me so angry. I bet he's so suspicious of us that he'll turn around to make sure we're not followin' him."

"Bet you he won't," said the younger, in a rare act of defiance.

"We'll see," said the elder. So they turned around and watched the lizard walk into the distance, waiting to see if he would turn around. They watched for many minutes, but the lizard disappeared around the distant bend without once looking back.

"Let's follow him to see if he turns his head now that he's safely out of sight," said the elder, and they followed and followed for miles and miles, but never once did the lizard turn around.

Suddenly, the elder possum broke off a tree branch, ran up behind the lizard and struck him on the head many times until the lizard was quite dead.

"Why did you do that?" asked the younger. "He didn't turn around. He didn't act like we were bad."

"Ah, he was thinkin' it," said the elder.

The Starving Sharks

The famine under the sea was getting chronic, even for the sharks. Paolo and Pedro swam around together as they always did, looking ever harder for things to eat.

They were able to survive for a while, but after several weeks the food shortage got so bad they grew thin and weak and their rib cages began to show.

"I'm absolutely starving, and that's not a figure of speech," said Pedro.

"Me too," said Paolo. "There's just nothing left to eat."

"Hey, I've got an idea," said Pedro. "We'd cover more ground if we searched separately. Let's split up and meet back here in an hour. I'll tell you what I find and you tell me what you find. Then we can share."

"Like we always do," said Paolo.

"Like we always do," said Pedro.

So they went their separate ways and met again an hour later.

"Bummer," said Pedro. "All I found was a bunch of other sharks looking for something to eat. What about you?"

"I found a container ship that must have just sunk," said Paolo. "It's full of food! Let's go."

They swam as fast as they could to the shipwreck only

to find that a group of other hungry sharks had already eaten everything.

"I am so sorry," said Pedro. "If you hadn't come back to tell me about all the food you could have feasted on it and saved yourself."

"If I'd done that you never would have forgiven me."

"But I would have understood."

"Why?"

"Because you would have lived on."

"Without you?"

Sharks don't usually cry, but Pedro couldn't help himself.

T H E   M E M O R Y   T E S T

A young woman visited an old people's home to see what the old people wanted to be remembered for after they died.

She went to the first person she saw.

"What do you want to be remembered for, old man?" she asked.

The old man regaled her with grand stories of all the adventures in his life. "That's what I want to be remembered for. My adventures."

She then went to an older man and asked what he wanted to be remembered for. He told her of his great achievements and discoveries.

"That's what I want to be remembered for. My achievements."

She then went to a man who was older still and asked: "What do you want to be remembered for?" He told her longingly and lovingly about the romantic life he had enjoyed. "That's what I want to be remembered for. My conquests."

Just as the young woman was about to leave, she noticed a man, even older than the men she had spoken to, sitting in a lonely corner. She went to him and asked: "What do you want to be remembered for?"

It took him a long time to reply. She thought he must have been either deaf or senile. Then he said something. It was a mumble at first, then a mutter. As she moved closer and closer to hear, the old, old man tried harder and harder to make himself understood. Eventually, she heard these words: "I just want to be remembered. I just want to be missed." Then he fell silent.

Seventy years later, the woman, now very old herself, thought back to that day and of the people she had spoken to. The only one she could remember anything about was the one who had told her nothing about his life, except that he wanted to be remembered and missed. And she did miss him, the way she hoped to be missed after her death, which was now not very far away.

THE SYMPATHY SHOP

Whenever people were in the market for some sympathy they went to Old Nick's Sympathy Shop in the mall. Whether it was for themselves or for someone else, they knew Old Nick's would have whatever sympathy they were after.

Old Nick had a wide variety of sympathy on offer. There was long-term sympathy and short-term sympathy. He had sympathy that could be applied quickly, and slow sympathy that would grow with the years. There was vintage sympathy and mass-produced sympathy. He had work-related sympathy and a wide range of sympathy suitable for domestic use. He could even whip up special one-off brands of sympathy, out the back.

Sympathy could be purchased singly, in six-packs or in slabs. There were party packs of sympathy, roll-on bottles of sympathy, vacuum-sealed cartons of sympathy (which would keep for years in a storage cupboard), liquid sympathy and spray cans of sympathy that were ozone-friendly.

"You always have so much sympathy in stock," said one of his many satisfied customers one fine, sunny day. "Where do you get it all from?"

"We make it right here on the premises," said Old Nick, "out the back."

One day, a regular customer asked if, along with sympathy, Old Nick stocked any sincerity.

"Sorry," said Old Nick. "No such thing as a sincerity shop." The customer's face dropped. Old Nick didn't like his customers to be unhappy.

"Tell you what. If I distill the extracts from some of my discontinued lines of sympathy, I reckon I could knock out a batch of synthetic sincerity for you to take home and try, no charge."

"Thanks," said the customer.

A week later the customer returned.

"How'd the syntho-sincerity go?" asked Old Nick.

"Not very well," said the customer. "People could tell. Don't you have any of the real stuff?"

"Afraid not," said Nick. "You have to grow that stuff yourself."

"Bugger," said the customer.

THE RAGGED GIRL AND THE ROCK

The stomach of the ragged girl grumbled loudly for the thousandth time that night. She was starving, so she went to a fast-food outlet and begged for scraps.

"We don't give handouts," said the fast-food-store proprietor.

"But if I don't eat something I'll starve," said the ragged girl.

"Like I care," said the fast-food proprietor, who then slammed the door in the ragged girl's face.

Feeling the bite of the cold, the ragged girl went to the house of a rich woman, hoping for some shelter.

"Get the hell out of here before I call the police," she said.

"But if I don't get some shelter, I'll die from the cold," said the ragged girl.

"Like I care," said the rich woman, who shut the door in the ragged girl's face.

As she walked away a police car pulled up alongside the ragged girl and took her in for vagrancy.

At the police station, the ragged girl was put in a cell with a policeman who proceeded to beat her up with a phone book.

"Please stop, or you'll kill me," said the ragged girl.

"Like I care," said the policeman, who then drove the ragged girl out to the backwoods and dumped her.

Tired, cold, hungry and bruised, the ragged girl walked along the bank of a small stream and saw what looked like a piece of food under a large rock. She reached under the rock to get the food, but the rock moved and caught her hand, trapping her. Just then it began to rain and the level of the water started to rise. It looked like the ragged girl was going to drown.

"Help, help," she yelled.

By sheer chance a hiker happened by and raised the alarm. To the ragged girl's aid came the fast-food proprietor, the rich woman and the policeman. They pushed the rock off her and saved the ragged girl from drowning.

"Thank you," said the ragged girl. "You saved my life."

"Well, we couldn't just let you die," they said.

Later that night she visited them all again, for exactly the same reasons. And each time she told them of her troubles, they all looked at her and said:

"Like I care."

CHELSEA STARLET'S RESTING PLACE

There was not a man alive who did not want to have immediate sex with Chelsea Starlet, for Chelsea Starlet was the most desirable woman in the world.

Chelsea was not a remarkable career woman. She worked as a third-class clerk in a large corporation and was not all that interested in her job. But that did not stop the high-powered executives in their plush, air-conditioned offices, twenty-seven floors above where Chelsea worked, from making the lamest of excuses to go down to her department just to have one quick glance at her.

It also did not matter that she had such an ordinary job. The line of men vying for Chelsea Starlet's attentions and affections would have stretched across three postcodes, and each and every one of those men would have devoted their lives to her, if only she would let them.

Unfortunately for all these men, Chelsea Starlet was also smart. She knew what she had and had no intention of settling for second best.

"It's going to have to be a very special man that gets near these goodies," she would confide to herself each morning in front of the mirror, as she slipped into yet another stunning outfit that was bound to drive every man she passed in the street and every man in the office limp with desire.

A lot of men did get near Chelsea Starlet's goodies, although they never got quite as close as they wanted to. This was because Chelsea had standards. If there was one tiny thing she didn't like about any of her wannabe beaux, they'd be out the door before their hormones hit second gear.

The years went by and Chelsea Starlet's allure grew and grew, along with the population of men who wanted to love her and provide for her and cherish her. But although many got close to her, none managed to win her over.

One by one the army of Chelsea Starlet disciples got married and reluctantly went on with their own lives. This was fine with Chelsea because she was willing to wait.

This she did until she was old and decrepit.

One bitter winter's morning a passer-by saw Chelsea Starlet shivering in the gutter.

"Why are you cold and starving and lying in the gutter?" the person asked.

"Because my standards are so high," said Chelsea Starlet.

What the Gnu Knew

Life in the jungle had got so bad that a bunch of animals just up and left. They cordoned off a quiet little corner of the jungle and declared it their own.

While the rest of the jungle continued to stew in turmoil, the dissident animals managed a workable peace by abiding by one simple rule: that it was not necessary to like one another, just to tolerate one another. This was the dictum that kept the peace.

The dissident animals were administered by a special council, each member of which represented a value held dear by all the animals. The lion represented courage; the chimpanzee, religion; the elephant, family stability; the owl, wisdom; and the hippopotamus, dignity.

The council declared that the best way to preserve peace was to keep to themselves and not mix at all with the animals in the rest of the jungle, who, they said, would cause nothing but trouble.

The rest of the animals agreed and everything was fine.

Until a sparrow flew into their midst. The sparrow was not from another part of the jungle, but from far, far away. She was just a traveller exploring the world. One lazy Sunday afternoon the sparrow fell into idle conversation with a lowly gnu, who was chewing on some grass.

"That's quite a collection of bozos you got running this joint," said the sparrow.

"Mind your own business," said the gnu without looking up. "They do a good job, they keep us together, they keep the peace."

"Yeah, well I got news for you, gnu," said the sparrow. "The lion is a coward, the chimp is an atheist, the elephant's been divorced four times and is paying major alimony, the owl is an idiot and the hippo used to earn a living by having mud pies thrown at him in a travelling sideshow."

"You lie," said the gnu.

So the sparrow took the gnu to the forbidden parts of the jungle from where all the dissident animals had come. She proved to the gnu beyond any doubt that all the things she had said were true.

Once the gnu returned home the sparrow had something to say.

"You think you've got it so good here," the sparrow said. "You think those jerks represent something. You're living a lie." Then the sparrow flew off, leaving the gnu to ponder what he should do.

If he revealed what he knew, the animals would revolt, peace would die and chaos would reign, just like everywhere else in the jungle. If he didn't, peace would remain, but it would be based on countless horrible lies.

After many sleepless nights the gnu came to this conclusion: that the falsehoods were grotesque, but the peace was real.

So the gnu kept all the sparrow had told him to himself.

The gnu knew that what he did was wrong. But he also knew that what he did was right.

The Alchemist

A fable about following your dream
Paulo Coelho

The Alchemist is the magical story of Santiago, an Andalusian shepherd boy who yearns to travel in search of a worldly treasure as extravagant as any ever found. From his home in Spain he journeys to the markets of Tangiers and into the Egyptian desert where a fateful encounter with the alchemist awaits him.

This is a story that teaches us, as only few stories can, about the essential wisdom of listening to our hearts, learning to read the omens strewn along life's path, and above all, following our dreams.

Paulo Coelho is one of the most loved writers in Latin America. He is the author of five bestsellers.

ISBN 0062502182
$17.95

HarperCollins*Publishers*

The Pilgrimage

A contemporary quest for ancient wisdom
Paulo Coelho

The Pilgrimage recounts the spectacular trials of Paulo Coelho and his mysterious mentor, Petrus, as they journey across Spain in search of a miraculous sword – on a legendary road travelled by pilgrims of San Tiago since the Middle Ages. Part adventure story, part guide to self-mastery, this compelling tale delivers a powerful brew of magic and insight.

'An exciting tale.'
– *Library Journal*

Paulo Coelho's books, led by *The Alchemist*, have won numerous awards and have become permanent fixtures on bestseller lists in Brazil and around the world.

ISBN 006251279X
$19.95

HarperCollins*Publishers*

The Valkyries

An encounter with angels
Paulo Coelho

The story of *The Valkyries* begins when Paulo's mysterious master, J., gives him the seemingly impossible task of finding his guardian angel. Paulo and his wife Chris pack their bags and take off on a forty-day adventure in the Mojave Desert where they encounter more than they bargained for, including the Valkyries – a band of bold, leather-clad women travelling the desert on motorcycles, spreading the word of angels.

Much of the story is experienced through the eyes of Chris, who learns how to converse with her angel, beginning her own transformational journey down the path of magic. *The Valkyries* is a story of spiritual growth in which Paulo and Chris learn first-hand the lesson of *The Alchemist*: follow your dream.

Paulo Coelho lives in Rio de Janeiro.

ISBN 0732256267
$17.95

HarperCollins*Publishers*